Meet
Oprah
Winfrey

Meet
Oprah
Winfrey

by Audreen Buffalo

A Bullseye Biography

Random House New York

Photo credits: AP/Wide World Photos, p. 2, 6, 8, 10–14, 18, 24–25, 48, 57, 73, 76–78, 80, 83, 88, 90, 92, 94–96, 99, 102–105; Star File: Scott/Star File, 84; Shaw/Star File, 31, 100; Zuffante/Star File, 91, 106.

Cover design by Fabia Wargin Design and Creative Media Applications, Inc.
Published in the United States by Random House, Inc., New York, and simultaneously in Canada by Random House of Canada Limited, Toronto.
Library of Congress Cataloging-in-Publication Data
Buffalo, Audreen.
Meet Oprah Winfrey / by Audreen Buffalo.
    p. cm. — (A Bullseye biography)
ISBN 0-679-85425-8
1. Winfrey, Oprah—Juvenile literature. 2. Television personalities—United States—Biography—Juvenile literature. 3. Motion picture actors and actresses—United States—Biography—Juvenile literature. [1. Winfrey, Oprah. 2. Television personalities. 3. Actors and actresses. 4. Afro-Americans—Biography. 5. Women—Biography.] I. Title. II. Series.
PN1992.4.W56B84 1993
791.43'028'092—dc20
[B]   93-36000
Manufactured in the United States of America   10 9 8 7 6 5 4 3 2 1

Contents

As usual, Oprah has her audience spellbound.

1
Meet Oprah Winfrey

It is five o'clock in the morning. It is barely light outside. Oprah Winfrey wakes up and gets out of bed. She puts on her brightly colored jogging suit; then she puts on her running shoes. She heads for the indoor track, where she runs every morning.

Oprah says exercise is the best way for her to start the day. It helps her build energy for the many things she has to do. Oprah's

*Oprah discusses dieting with her audience as
she stands next to an exercise machine.*

life is very busy. But she likes it that way.

In the morning, Oprah will tape her TV program—"The Oprah Winfrey Show." In the afternoon, she will meet with her staff to plan new shows. She will also meet with people who have ideas for movies and TV specials. And there are meetings to decide where Oprah will appear. Then there is the work she does with children who live in a Chicago housing project.

But right now Oprah tries not to think about the day ahead. She is busy exercising. Once she has finished her workout and her breakfast, she is ready for a full day's work.

Oprah is in her makeup chair by 7:00. Her hairdresser and makeup person are ready. Everything moves very quickly now.

While Oprah is deciding what to wear on her talk show, her hairdresser puts her hair in

rollers. Then her makeup man brushes her
face with powder and blush. He applies lip-
stick with a small, thin brush. While all this
is going on, a producer enters the room to

Oprah asks for quiet from the crowd at Southwestern High School in Baltimore during the taping of her show.

brief Oprah on the day's taping. He reminds Oprah who the day's guests are.

Oprah already knows most of what her producer is telling her. She has done her

11

homework. Each night before she goes to
bed, she goes over her notes for the next
day's show.

Oprah in action on "The Oprah Winfrey Show." Here she holds the microphone out to a member of the audience in Cumming, Georgia.

Even so, Oprah listens carefully. She wants to make sure she has missed nothing. She also needs to know about last-minute

13

Oprah on the set of her show in 1988.

changes. Oprah wants everything to go smoothly.

She reminds herself that the studio audience must be part of the show. The people who come to see "The Oprah Winfrey Show" have helped make Oprah a star. Oprah knows that their ideas and opinions are very important. The audience must always feel that Oprah is a friend, as well as a talk show host. And Oprah really *does* care about her audience.

Finally, Oprah's hair and makeup are in shape. She is wearing a red suit and black shoes. The producer has finished giving her her notes. She is ready to head down to the studio.

Oprah strides quickly through the halls. She can already hear applause coming from the studio, where the audience is waiting.

Someone hands her a microphone. Oprah Winfrey walks down the aisle and stops in the middle of the audience. The whole audience is standing up and applauding. Oprah turns to face the special guests who are seated on the stage. They are all ready for her first question.

"The Oprah Winfrey Show" begins!

2
Farm Girl

Today, Oprah Winfrey is a very happy and successful TV star, actress, and producer. But she worked very hard to become what she is. Oprah got into a lot of trouble when she was growing up. This is the story of how she grew up and how she became the person she is today.

Oprah Gail Winfrey was born on January 29, 1954. She was born on a small farm in Kosciusko, Mississippi. Her mother,

*Oprah proudly accepts the 1987 award for Outstanding
Talk/Service Show Host at the 14th Annual
Daytime Emmy Awards.*

Vernita Lee, had been raised on that farm. Oprah's father, Vernon Winfrey, was a soldier who was stationed at a nearby army base. Both of Oprah's parents were very young when she was born. They never married each other.

Miss Vernita Lee had wanted to name her baby "Orpah," after a woman in the Bible. But someone had made a mistake on the baby's birth certificate. They switched the *r* and the *p*. The baby's name appeared as "Oprah." Miss Lee kept it that way, and Oprah never changed it.

After Oprah was born, her mother tried to look for work. But she could not find a job in the small town of Kosciusko. So Miss Lee moved to Milwaukee, Wisconsin, to work as a maid. She left little Oprah to be cared for by *her* mother, Hattie Mae Lee.

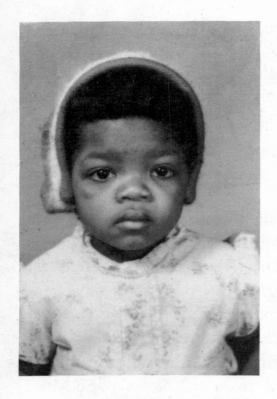

A two-year-old Oprah poses for a church photo in Kosciusko, Mississippi.

Hattie Mae lived on a farm in Kosciusko. It was just like the farm that Oprah's mother had grown up on. And since there is always work to do on a farm, Hattie Mae gave Oprah many chores.

One of Oprah's jobs was to feed the chickens. Oprah didn't mind. She liked the way the chickens rushed to greet her with noisy cackles each time she entered the barnyard. Oprah also tended the pigs and took the cows out to the pasture.

But Oprah was a very lonely girl. No children lived nearby. Oprah's only playmates were a corncob doll her mother had given her and the chickens, pigs, and cows. So Oprah often gave them parts in the games and plays she made up.

Sundays were different from every other day on the farm. After the morning chores were done, Hattie Mae would pack a picnic lunch. Then she and Oprah would get dressed in their Sunday best and head for church. They belonged to the Buffalo United Methodist Church.

First, Oprah would go to Sunday school, where there were boys and girls her age. For the next two hours, Oprah was happy to spend time with the other children and learn stories and lessons from the Bible. After Sunday school was over, Oprah would join her grandmother for the morning service. Singing, sermons, and the soft, *swiisshh*-ing sound of hand-held fans filled the church. It was often very hot inside the church. The grownups tried to cool off by fanning themselves. Oprah wanted a fan, too, but Hattie Mae said that waving one just made you warmer.

The service went on for three long hours. Oprah tried very hard to sit still and listen to the sermon. But that was not always easy. So

Oprah's mind would wander. She liked to watch the three wasps' nests that were just beneath the ceiling fan. She wondered what the wasps were up to. She would imagine what would happen if the wasps got angry and left their nests during the service!

Sometimes Oprah played "let's pretend." She would sit very quietly next to her grandmother. But her mind would travel to the places and people she had learned about in Sunday School. Oprah made up questions she wanted to ask the people from the stories in the Bible. Sometimes she thought up new plays for her corncob doll and her barnyard friends.

When the service ended at 2:30, everyone would gather on the church lawn. The adults unpacked their picnic baskets and talked about the sermon, the singing, and the local

news. Oprah ran and played with the other boys and girls. The children were happy to be free from the hard wooden seats and the

In 1989 Oprah opened a restaurant called The Eccentric in Chicago. Here she and her employees celebrate its opening.

watchful eyes of the grownups.

Soon it was time to eat the delicious food. Everyone had brought enough food to share.

Sometimes the women exchanged recipes.

Then, at four o'clock, everyone returned to church for the evening service.

Church was a very important part of Oprah's life when she was growing up.

3

"Little Miss Winfrey Will Recite"

Life on the farm wasn't just chores and going to church. There was also much learning to do. Hattie Mae read to Oprah every day. She taught her to recognize letters and the sounds they made. So by the time Oprah was three, she was reading!

Oprah also learned how to write. On her first day in school, she wrote a note to her kindergarten teacher. The note said: "Dear

Miss New, I do not think I belong here."
Miss New agreed. Oprah was placed in first
grade. And at the end of her first school year,

Oprah kids around with actor Robin Williams after the 1987 taping of an episode of her show at the Comic Relief benefit. Looking on are actors Billy Crystal (second from left) and Dudley Moore.

she was skipped to third grade.

Oprah had also begun to memorize and recite poems when she was very young. She made her first appearance at a church Easter program when she was only three years old. At Christmas, she was asked to recite again. Whenever a tea, recital, or special Sunday school program was planned, Oprah was one of the first children asked to recite.

Oprah can remember the women in church fanning themselves and saying, "Hattie Mae, that child sure is gifted." And by the time she was four, everyone in town knew that Oprah was gifted. They began to call her "the little speaker."

Oprah liked learning the poems she would recite. She liked making them come alive. But most of all, Oprah loved being on stage. She could hardly wait for the person in charge of the program to announce, "Little Miss Winfrey will now do her recitation." Then Oprah would walk on stage and recite

Oprah looking great—as usual.

her poem. Sometimes she would curtsy when she was finished. Sometimes she would bow.

Many children get nervous when they have to perform. But Oprah always felt comfortable on stage. She felt as if she truly belonged there. People told her that she had a beautiful voice. She made the poems she read sound special. She loved knowing that everyone wanted to hear her speak.

Oprah became very popular. She recited at church banquets, before women's groups, and at teas and recitals. When someone asked young Oprah what she wanted to do when she grew up, she would say, "I want to be paid to talk."

But when she was at home with her grandmother, Oprah had to be silent when adults were around.

"Children," she was told, "should be seen

and not heard." But Oprah was a lively, talkative little girl. She liked attention and company. She did *not* like Hattie Mae's rule. Besides, she knew that everyone loved to hear her speak at church. So she did not understand why her grandmother did not want her to speak at home. It was hard for Oprah to obey her grandmother. And when she disobeyed, she was punished. Her grandmother would whip her with a switch. Oprah still remembers today the pain of this punishment. She also remembers how she would copy her grandmother and whip her dolls.

To add to her misery, Oprah started wishing, at a very young age, that she were white instead of black. She saw white children with more toys, fancier clothes, and bigger houses. And of course she wanted these things, too.

So it's not surprising that she felt the way she did. She even wore a clothespin on her nose to try to make it grow narrower, like the white children's noses. Later, she would be very proud that she was black.

Oprah soon left the farm in Kosciusko. And even though her grandmother was so very strict, some of Oprah's fondest memories are of those early years in Mississippi.

She still thinks about the farm and how she made the chickens, cows, and pigs her friends. She remembers the green of the church lawn. She remembers the Sunday picnics. She thinks back to the times she sat with her head close to Hattie Mae's as she learned the sound the letter *q* made. She smiles at the memory of a poem she recited at a Sunday school tea.

But most of all, Oprah remembers sitting

on her grandmother's lap on the front porch during a thunderstorm. Hattie Mae held her tight and told her how God protects his children. Oprah remembers how safe she felt.

4

Going to the City

When Oprah was six years old, her mother decided that she was now ready to take care of her. So Oprah left Hattie Mae's. This was exciting but also a little scary for Oprah. The farm had been her whole life. But Oprah looked forward to living with her mother in a big city. That city was Milwaukee, Wisconsin.

Oprah soon found that life in Milwaukee with her mother was very different from life on the farm. Oprah had never been in such a noisy, crowded place with so many different types of people. She had never seen so many buildings and streets before. Oprah was curious about everything she saw in the city. She wanted to go to the movies. She wanted to wear the pretty clothes she saw in the store windows. She asked her mother to buy her the toys she saw the other children playing with.

But Vernita had very little money. She could not afford to buy the clothes and toys Oprah wanted. She and Oprah had to live in one room in another woman's house.

There was another problem, too. Vernita couldn't always be with Oprah. She had to work very hard for long hours. So she left Oprah with her cousin Alice and sometimes with a neighbor. And when she came

*Oprah helps decorate the family
Christmas tree in Nashville.*

home at night, she was too tired to give Oprah the attention she needed. Oprah was too young to understand how hard her mother worked. Instead, she was angry at her mother for being away so much. She began to talk back to her mother and to disobey her.

Vernita saw that Oprah was unhappy living in Milwaukee. So she sent Oprah to Nashville to spend time with her father, who was now married. Vernon and Zelma Winfrey welcomed Oprah into their home. And Oprah was happy to be with her father. But she also found that her father and stepmother expected her to obey their rules.

There were chores to do around the house. Oprah had to help wash the dishes. She had to make her bed and keep her room neat. And each Sunday, Mr. and Mrs. Winfrey took Oprah to church. Oprah went to Bible classes and performed in Sunday school programs and at recitals. She was happy to be on stage once again.

Mr. and Mrs. Winfrey knew Oprah was very good at reading, writing, and speaking. But they found out that her arithmetic skills needed a good deal of work. So each morning before he went to work, Mr. Winfrey left a page of addition and subtraction problems on the kitchen table for Oprah to solve. Then he would drill her on the arithmetic questions each night.

One day, Oprah's mother called with exciting news. She was going to have a baby! Oprah would now have a half brother or sister. And Vernita wanted Oprah to come back to Milwaukee and live there with the two of them in a house instead of in one room. She felt that maybe now she would be able to make a good life for Oprah.

Oprah was excited at the thought of having a baby brother or sister. But she was also a little bit afraid. She was used to being the only child in the house. Now she would have to share her mother with someone she did not know. Would she like the baby? Would the baby like her?

Oprah missed her mother. And it would be different living with her in a house, instead of sharing a room in someone else's house. The more Oprah thought about this new life, the more excited she became. She began to like the idea of having a brother or sister to play with.

Mr. and Mrs. Winfrey were sad. But they tried not to show it. They wanted Oprah to stay with them. They liked having her with them. But Mr. and Mrs. Winfrey felt they had to honor her mother's wishes. "It's only fair," they told each other. They just wanted Oprah to be happy.

5

We Are a Family

Oprah moved back to Milwaukee. Her mother gave birth to a girl. Now Oprah had a half sister. And she and her sister and mother all lived together.

At first, things were fine. Everyone was learning about one another. But Oprah's mother still had to go to work every day. And even though Oprah played with her sister, she still felt lonely and unhappy.

Oprah wanted more attention from her

mother, especially when she had another baby two years later. Now Oprah had a half brother as well. Oprah felt that her mother liked the other children better and paid more attention to them. She also felt that her mother liked her sister better since she had lighter skin. Oprah's mother said that wasn't true. She told Oprah that she treated them all the same way. But Oprah didn't feel that way. She got into arguments with her brother and sister. Sometimes they wouldn't even speak to her and she wouldn't speak to them. Sometimes they just went off to play with their friends and left her alone.

Because Oprah was unhappy, she began to misbehave. She stayed out when she was supposed to be at home. And she made up stories.

One day when she was nine years old,

Oprah saw some glasses with beautiful blue frames in a store window. She begged her mother to buy them. She asked her every day for a week. Oprah didn't need new glasses, her mother said. Her old glasses were fine. But Oprah just had to have those glasses. So she broke her own glasses and made up a story. When Vernita came home from work, Oprah showed her the broken glasses. She said that burglars had broken into the house and knocked her unconscious. Oprah told her mother that the glasses had broken when she fell. Vernita knew that Oprah was lying.

But that didn't keep Oprah from making up more stories.

Oprah very much wanted a puppy. But her mother wouldn't let her have one. She already had her hands full with three children to care for! Then, one day, a puppy followed Oprah home. This gave Oprah an idea.

First, she threw her mother's jewelry out the window. Then, when her mother came home, Oprah told her that burglars had broken into the house and stolen her jewelry. She said they had threatened her, too. They would have taken more, Oprah said. But a puppy had followed her home. And the brave little puppy had scared them off. Vernita did not believe this story either.

Then Oprah did something even worse. One day, she saw a famous singer getting out of a limousine. She walked up to her. She told the woman that relatives had left her in Milwaukee. She said she didn't know where her relatives had gone. She said she was from Ohio and didn't know anyone in Milwaukee. She cried and said she wanted to go home.

She said that she needed bus fare.

The famous singer believed Oprah's story. She gave Oprah $100 so she could go home to Ohio. Oprah took the money. She used it to stay in a nice hotel overnight.

Oprah's family looked all over the city for her, but they could not find her. Finally, the minister from Oprah's church found her. He brought her home. Her mother was very happy that Oprah had been found. But she was angry with Oprah, too.

It seemed by now that Oprah had enough problems. It seemed that nothing worse could happen to her. But it did. When Oprah was nine years old, a very bad thing happened to her. A nineteen-year-old cousin who was baby-sitting for her took advantage of her and abused her. He touched her in places that were private to her. What he did was

*In 1991 Oprah testified in Washington, D.C., before the
Senate Judiciary Committee against child abuse.*

against the law. But Oprah became confused. She was afraid to tell anyone.

So no one even knew what had happened to Oprah. In those days, people didn't talk about abuse. Children didn't know how to protect themselves as well as they do now. They often were afraid to tell anyone what had happened. Sometimes they blamed themselves. Oprah kept all her feelings inside. She didn't tell anyone. She didn't tell her mother, her father, or her teacher.

But when Oprah grew up, she decided to tell people what had happened to her. She told them so they would try to stop other people from abusing children. She wanted people to know that it wasn't their fault if this had happened to them. And she wanted children to learn that they can say "no."

Today Oprah works to help children and

women who have been abused. She knows that it is very important to help them. She understands how they feel.

Oprah became a very angry child. She continued to tell lies, play tricks on people, and even steal money from her mother. Vernita was finally at her wit's end. She didn't know what to do about Oprah. She could not make her behave. She wanted to be a good mother. But she didn't think she could help her daughter. She was worried that Oprah would get into serious trouble.

Finally, Vernita thought of a solution. She decided to send Oprah to a special home for girls who had a lot of problems. She hoped that the people at the home would be able to help Oprah.

Oprah was frightened. What kind of home would this be? What would they do to her there? Did this mean she would never see her mother again? Or her father and step-mother?

Oprah was almost fourteen years old by now. But she wished she was still a little girl sitting on her grandmother's lap. She wanted to feel Hattie Mae's arms around her. She wanted to hear her grandmother tell her again how God protects his children.

Vernita packed Oprah's bags. They went to see the people who would arrange for Oprah to go to the home. Vernita talked to a woman in the office for a long time. The woman made some phone calls. She talked to Vernita some more. Then the woman made another phone call. When she hung up, she looked at Vernita and shook her head.

The home was too crowded. They had no room for Oprah!

The next day Mr. Winfrey called. Over

the phone, Oprah's mother, father, and step-mother agreed that Oprah would go back to live with her father and stepmother in Nashville.

Mr. and Mrs. Winfrey told Oprah how much they loved and missed her. But they also said that she would have to change her ways. Oprah would have to live by the rules of their house, as she had done when she was younger.

Oprah wasn't exactly sure what changing her ways might mean. But she was ready to give it a try.

6

Oprah and Her Father

Oprah and her father and stepmother had to get to know each other all over again. Oprah seemed very different from the little girl who had lived with them before. She wore clothes that Vernon and Zelma felt were too old for her. She seemed to have forgotten her manners, too.

The first thing Mr. Winfrey did was to set up some rules for Oprah.

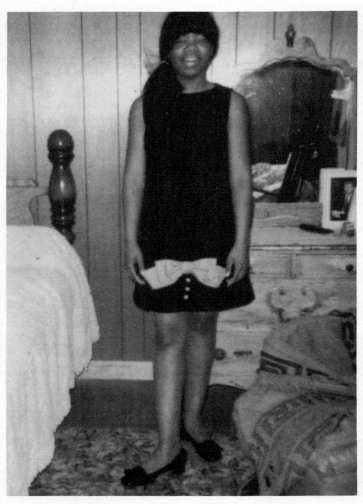

*Dressed in her finest, a teenage Oprah poses
in her bedroom in Nashville.*

His first rule was that she should call him "Dad." She should not call him "Pops." He didn't say it, but Oprah knew he thought that "Pops" was rude.

Next, the very short skirts Oprah wore when she arrived at the Winfreys' had to go. Oprah's father and stepmother felt that short skirts were not appropriate for a fourteen-year-old girl. So Zelma Winfrey bought Oprah some new dresses. Oprah didn't want to wear them. She said they made her look like a baby. But Mr. and Mrs. Winfrey said that Oprah would have to dress her age.

Oprah did not question her father's rules for long. She knew he meant everything he said. She had already disobeyed her mother. And she felt bad about that. Now she did not want to do anything to displease her father.

Mr. Winfrey had three jobs. He was a

barber. He owned a general store. And he was a member of the Nashville City Council. He and the other members of the council wanted to make sure that Nashville was a good place to live. Part of their job was to solve the city's problems.

Oprah saw that Mr. Winfrey liked to work. And she soon realized that he expected her to work hard, too. He knew that Oprah was smart. With a little hard work, he felt Oprah could be whatever she wanted.

One of Mr. Winfrey's rules was that Oprah had to learn five new words every day. She had to pick the words from the dictionary and study their meanings. Then, each night before supper, Mr. Winfrey would ask Oprah what words she had learned that day.

Oprah would stand at the dining-room

Oprah poses with her favorite book in a pro-reading poster
published by the American Library Association.

table and recite the list of words she had chosen. Mr. Winfrey would ask her to spell each one. Then he would ask her to use each one in a sentence. If Oprah had not done her word work, she would not be allowed to eat supper. Oprah didn't want to miss supper. So she was always prepared.

Oprah began to look forward to the dictionary tests. She became a word explorer. She searched for words that many people didn't know. She tried to find words that even her teachers didn't know.

Mr. Winfrey also insisted that Oprah read a new book every week. Then she had to write a book report about it. This wasn't too difficult for Oprah because she loved to read.

Oprah was a good student. She studied hard and did her homework. Some of her

Oprah's high school yearbook photo.

good study habits may have come from her love for her fourth-grade teacher in Milwaukee, Mrs. Duncan. Oprah says today that

Mrs. Duncan was one of the most important people in her life. Oprah admired her so much that for quite some time she wanted to become a fourth-grade teacher. For Mrs. Duncan, Oprah always handed in her papers early.

Oprah liked her high school. It was called Nashville East High School. Oprah's teachers also liked her. She was happy with the work she was doing. Her good manners had returned. And she was friendly with the other boys and girls.

East High School had an excellent class in public speaking. Naturally, Oprah signed up for it. She was still being asked to speak before church groups and at official civic dinners. And by now she was not only reciting poems, she was writing speeches of her own, too. She knew the class would help her to become even more skilled at speaking in public.

Many women's groups wanted Oprah to speak at their gatherings. Sometimes Oprah traveled on church outings to other cities. Sometimes she went just to give a speech. Once, she even won $500 in a contest for a speech she had given before a woman's club.

Oprah also joined the high school drama club. She liked everything about the club. There was lots of activity. Everyone pitched in to build the scenery. The noise of hammering and laughter filled the hall. The smell of paint was all around.

Oprah liked trying out for the parts she most wanted to play. She liked to see if the teacher picked her for the parts. Sometimes she would get the part she wanted. Sometimes she would be asked to play another

Oprah as a young lady in Nashville.

part. And it was easy for Oprah to learn her lines. After all, she had been memorizing poems since she was a small child.

Oprah liked appearing on stage most of all. She liked wearing costumes and stage make-up. She couldn't wait for her turn to take the stage. And she liked the applause at the final curtain.

In her last year of high school, Oprah decided her career would have something to do with speaking or drama.

During that year Oprah was elected president of the high school student council. And, later that year, she was invited to the White House Conference on Youth. This meant that she would travel to Colorado, where she would meet with high school students from all over the country. Oprah and the rest of the students met with President Nixon. The president told them that he was proud of what good students and citizens they were. Oprah was thrilled to go on this special trip and meet the president.

Oprah had changed a lot in the three years since she had come from Milwaukee. Later that year, Oprah was invited to Los Angeles on a speaking engagement. She saw many of the famous Hollywood movie studios. Being in Hollywood made Oprah think about how much she liked her drama class. Wouldn't it be great to work in the movie business? she thought. But Oprah wasn't ready yet to decide on exactly what career she would choose.

Oprah's last year of high school was very exciting. She had met the president and she had been to Hollywood. She had even been crowned Miss Fire Prevention of

Nashville. Her life had become very full and happy. But it was time to think about college.

When Oprah and her father sat down to talk about college, Mr. Winfrey told Oprah he thought she should go to Tennessee State University. The school was nearby and Oprah could live at home. But of course there was the expense of college.

Then Oprah heard about a big speech contest the Elks held every year in Nashville. The first prize was a scholarship to Tennessee State University. Oprah entered the contest— and won! The scholarship would pay Oprah's expenses at college. She would start at TSU the next semester.

One day, while Oprah was still a senior in high school, her drama class visited a local radio station, WVOL. A disc jockey asked

Oprah if she would like to hear her voice on the radio. Oprah said sure! So she read the news for them. All the station executives loved how Oprah's voice sounded. They loved it so much that they offered her a job reading the news and weather on the air! Two months before she graduated from high school, Oprah was hired by WVOL.

The work came easily to Oprah. She was a good reader. But she had to learn the director's signals. The signals told her when to begin speaking and when to break for a commercial. And they told her when the newscast was over.

Every day after school, Oprah went to her job at station WVOL. This was the beginning of her career. People all over Nashville would hear Oprah's voice!

When Oprah started at TSU that September, she had a very busy schedule. She had to learn all about the college. She had to study very hard. And she was still working at the radio station. But she decided to enter the Miss Black Tennessee Contest. And she won! What a long way Oprah had come since the days in Kosciusko when she had wished she were white. Now she was proud of who she was.

Soon a local television station offered Oprah a job. But she turned it down. Maybe she thought she had enough to do already. But Oprah's speech professor was surprised. She thought the job could be a wonderful chance for Oprah to find out what it would be like to work in television. Learning about different careers is one of the reasons people go to college, she told Oprah.

Oprah thought it over once again. She

One of Oprah's many honors and accomplishments as a young woman was to become Miss Black Tennessee.

decided to take the job. And so she quit her job at WVOL and became a TV anchor-woman at age nineteen.

Oprah was able to fit everything into her busy schedule. This was because she was a very organized person. She thought every-thing through first. Then she knew how she would tackle each task. This helped her get through college with good grades. And Oprah feels that being extra-organized helps her in her work today.

Mr. Winfrey continued to have strict rules about where Oprah could go. And about whom she could spend time with. Oprah was sure she was the only newswoman in the country who had to be home by 11:00 P.M.!

Oprah found this harder and harder to accept. She felt she was a grownup now. She had adult responsibilities. She was earning an adult's salary while she was still in college. Yet Mr. Winfrey continued to check on her grades. He wanted Oprah to do well in school, just as he had when she was younger. But Oprah didn't want to be treated like a child.

Oprah finally felt it was time for her to leave home and live on her own. She began to look around for another place to work, away from Nashville.

Then, just a few months before she was to graduate from college, Oprah was offered a full-time job at a television station. It was in Baltimore, Maryland. Baltimore was quite far from her father's house in Nashville— more than seven hundred miles away. So Oprah had to make a big decision. Should she leave school just two months before graduation? Or should she finish school and hope another offer would come along? In the end, Oprah decided the offer was too good to pass up. Oprah moved to Baltimore to take the job.

7

Away from Home

Oprah's new job called for her to be a television reporter. Oprah had never done this kind of work before. She had been an anchorwoman, not a reporter. Reporting was very different from reading the news from notes that someone else gave her. It was also different from making a speech about her own thoughts.

Reporters have to find out the facts. They must listen to both sides of the story. Then

Oprah at a news conference in Chicago in 1985, where it was announced that her current show, "A.M. Chicago," would be called "The Oprah Winfrey Show." Within a year, the show was broadcast to a nationwide audience.

they have to tell these facts to the people watching television.

A reporter is not supposed to let the audience know her own thoughts. One reason for this is to allow the people who are watching to make up their own minds.

Sometimes Oprah had to report a sad story. And sometimes it was hard for her to keep from crying. But reporters are not supposed to show their feelings. Oprah found it hard to keep her feelings inside when people were in trouble.

Once, Oprah's boss asked her to talk to a woman whose house had just burned down. Oprah did not want to do it. She knew the woman would be crying and very upset. Millions of TV viewers would be looking at her. Oprah didn't think it was fair to make the woman face cameras and a reporter after what had happened to her.

Oprah's boss told her she had to talk to the woman. If she didn't, she would lose her job. Oprah did it. But she felt ashamed that she had bothered the woman. The woman already had so many troubles.

Oprah went back to the studio and sat behind her desk. She looked at the tape of the news story. It showed Oprah asking the woman questions. Then it showed the woman talking to Oprah. The woman was very upset. Finally, the tape showed Oprah apologizing to the woman for asking so many questions when she was having such a hard time.

Oprah got into a lot of trouble. Her boss did not like the apology. Reporters are not supposed to apologize for doing their job.

But Oprah did not know how to "take herself out of the story." She would take sides. She would talk about the story as though it had happened to her.

Oprah says now that she was never a

good reporter. A reporter writes her own stories and reads them out loud. But Oprah
never liked writing her own stories and read-

In 1985 Oprah takes a moment to put her feet up in her studio office after a morning taping of "The Oprah Winfrey Show."

ing them out loud. She liked to "ad-lib," which means to decide what you will say as you are speaking.

Oprah has every reason to be happy, here in Los Angeles in 1986. Her talk show is about to be expanded to a national audience.

Oprah was fired from her job. She had never been fired from a job before. She was twenty-two years old.

But things weren't so very bad. Oprah's boss gave her another job. She would co-host a morning talk show called "People Are Talking." The other host was a man named Richard Sher. Oprah and Richard talked about a lot of different subjects on the show.

After just her first day on the job, Oprah knew deep down that this was the job she was made for. This was the first job where she could really be herself.

It was an important beginning for Oprah. In many ways, "People Are Talking" was very much like Oprah's show today.

Oprah was able to talk to people about the things that had happened in their lives. She talked to all kinds of people about all

In 1988 Oprah accepted the award for Broadcaster of the Year from Bill Greenwald, president of the International Radio and Television Society.

kinds of things. She could say what she thought. And she also wanted to know what the audience thought.

Oprah stayed with that show for seven years. It became very popular. Her boss was very pleased.

But soon Oprah decided it was time to move on.

She began to look for a bigger job, in a bigger city. She had always wanted to live in Chicago. Maybe now was her chance. She sent tapes of "People Are Talking" to a talk show in Chicago.

The people at the show, "A.M. Chicago," liked what they saw. They offered Oprah a job!

Oprah made "A.M. Chicago" so popular that the station expanded it from half an hour to an hour. Then they changed its name to "The Oprah Winfrey Show."

"The Oprah Winfrey Show" grew so quickly that people all over the country heard about it. More people wanted to see it. Before long the show was being shown in 130 cities. Today, more than 14 million people all across America watch the show.

"The Oprah Winfrey Show" is one of the most popular shows on TV. It has won five Emmy awards as the Best Television Talk Show. Oprah has also won three Emmy awards as Best Talk Show Host.

The Chicago station no longer owns "The Oprah Winfrey Show." Oprah does! She was the first person in history to own and produce her very own show. She even owns her own TV and film studio. Only two other women have ever owned their own studio. One was an actress named Mary Pickford. The other was Lucille Ball.

Oprah never forgot that she left college without her degree. Even though she was

Oprah beams as she accepts yet another Emmy Award.

Here she comes—Oprah Winfrey.

famous, she wanted that degree. For one thing, she knew it would please her father.

Oprah has never forgotten what her

father's caring and concern did for her. She tells everyone that her father's love and discipline saved her life.

When Oprah left college, she had completed all of her work except for one project. She wrote the school and asked if she could graduate if she finished the project. "Yes," they said.

Oprah did the work that was needed to get her diploma.

Eleven years after she left Tennessee State University, Oprah returned to get that diploma. The school asked if she would give a speech to the graduating class.

One of the many things Oprah said in her speech was this: "Every time I come home, my dad says, 'You need that degree.' So this is a special day for my dad."

Oprah also said that she was setting up a

scholarship program. It is called the Vernon Winfrey Scholarship Fund. Each year Oprah gives ten scholarships in her father's name to Tennessee State University.

8

A Movie Star

Oprah read a book that she liked a lot. She liked it so much that she gave copies of the book to all her friends. The book was called *The Color Purple*. It was written by Alice Walker. The book told the story of a group of black women and men who lived in the South. It is an adventure story about the struggles of each character.

Oprah hoped *The Color Purple* would be made into a movie. But she didn't know that

Oprah playing Sofia in The Color Purple.

a movie was already being planned. And one day, the co-producer of the movie came to Chicago. His name was Quincy Jones.

Quincy Jones was in Chicago on other business. He had to meet with his lawyer. While Mr. Jones was waiting for his lawyer, he turned on the TV set in his hotel room. Oprah's show was on.

Mr. Jones watched the entire show. Then he picked up the telephone and called Steven Spielberg. Mr. Spielberg was the director of *The Color Purple*. Mr. Jones told Mr. Spielberg that he had the right woman for the part.

Oprah will never forget what happened next. She says it was the most magical thing that had ever happened to her. Quincy Jones called her and told her that she would be perfect for a role in *The Color Purple*. He

Oprah and actor James Earl Jones pose together backstage after a performance of the play "Fences" in New York City.

asked her to audition for the part. And he said he would send her a script.

Oprah was terribly excited. Soon *The*

Color Purple was all she could think about. She worked hard to prepare herself for the audition. She studied the script. She read the book over and over again. Then she thought about all the characters. She thought about

Oprah poses with musicians Paul Simon (middle) and Quincy Jones. Jones helped Oprah get a part in the movie The Color Purple.

One of Oprah's television projects was "The Women of Brewster Place," a powerful two-part miniseries that aired in 1989.

where they lived. She thought about how they behaved toward each other. She studied the characters until they became people she knew well.

Oprah practiced reading from the script that Mr. Jones sent her. Then she auditioned. And she got the part! She took a short leave from "The Oprah Winfrey Show" to make the movie.

Oprah found that acting was difficult. She was playing a character named Sofia. Sofia is a funny and strong person who has had a hard time in her life. Oprah wondered how she could make an audience believe she was Sofia. Then she learned that acting is letting the spirit of the person you're playing come out. And that's just what Oprah did.

Oprah received an Academy Award nom-

Oprah with actress Faye Dunaway at the opening-night party for "From the Mississippi Delta," the first play Oprah produced (1991).

ination for her role as Sofia in *The Color Purple*. At that time, making her first movie was the high point of Oprah's life.

Oprah liked being in *The Color Purple* so much she began to think about making her own movies. She now has her own company that produces movies and television

"I won!" Oprah seems to be saying as she accepts the 1992 Emmy Award for Outstanding Talk/Service Show Host during the 19th Annual Daytime Emmy Awards.

Oprah and actor Denzel Washington (left) pose
as co-hosts of the 1992 Essence Awards.
With them is actor Kenny Black.

projects. She named it Harpo Productions. People often ask Oprah, "What does 'Harpo' mean?" She tells them they can find out if they write Harpo backward.

9

"If I Can Do It, So Can You!"

Oprah is very popular. People like her because she is very much like them. On her show, she talks about things people think about. She asks her guests to talk about happy and sad things that have happened to them and their families. Oprah tells them about things that have happened to her. She asks her guests how they really feel. She laughs with them. Sometimes she even cries

Oprah in 1992 with her familiar "thumbs-up" sign.

*Oprah with "Cosby kids" Raven-Symone (left)
and Keshia Knight Pulliam (right).*

with them. They know she cares about them.

Oprah always finds time to speak to groups of kids all over the country. She cares about young people. In the summer of 1993, Oprah's company shot a movie called *There Are No Children Here*. The movie is the true story of two boys struggling to grow up in a Chicago housing project. And the movie was filmed right at the housing project where the real story took place.

While she was making the movie, Oprah became friends with the children living in the housing project. So after she was done filming the movie, Oprah decided to set up both a tutoring program and a scholarship program for the children. It is called the Henry Horner Tutoring Program and Scholarship Fund.

Oprah has set up many other programs

Michael Jackson points out the sights to Oprah at his ranch in California.

for children. In 1985–1986, she ran a program called the Little Sisters of Cabrini-Green. She and some of her staff acted as Big

Sisters (*Khidaddas*) to girls who lived in Chicago's Cabrini-Green housing project.

The Little Sisters had lots of activities.

Sometimes there were sleepovers. Sometimes Oprah and her staff took the girls to movies and parties. But in order to stay in the Little

Oprah interviews Michael Jackson in a live one-on-one interview in 1993.

Sisters, the girls had to get good grades. They could not get C's and D's. Oprah paid a lot of attention to those grades. She pays the

Oprah says good-bye after another exciting day.

same attention to the students who apply for the scholarships to Tennessee State University. She chooses each student very carefully.

It's important to Oprah that kids feel good about themselves. She often tells them stories of what has happened in her life. "I want my work to make people feel special," she says.

Whenever Oprah talks to kids, she emphasizes one thing. It is the message of the story that you've just read: "If I can do it, so can you."

AUDREEN BUFFALO has worked as an editor at several major magazines, including *Redbook*, *Essence*, and *Lear's*. She is currently an editor at *Mirabella* magazine. This is her first book for children. Ms. Buffalo lives in Riverdale, New York City.

Bullseye Biographies